YOUR HOUSE IS NOT JUST A HOUSE

Words by Idris Goodwin • Art by Lorraine Nam

CLARION BOOKS
An Imprint of HarperCollinsPublishers

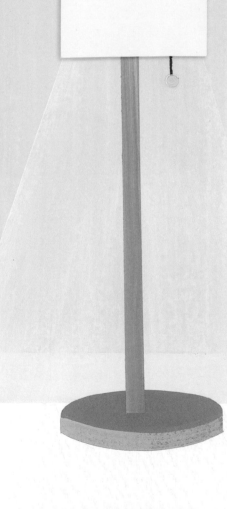

For the children —I.G.

For Jon —L.N.

It seems your home is just
walls, windows, and doors . . .

but take a closer look—
    it's that and so much more.

That closet is not a closet—
it's a teleportation chamber

that will take you to a planet
with robots screaming, *Danger!*

That couch is not a couch—
it's the top rope of a ring

and you're a masked wrestling champion—
the Unbearable Terrible Scream!

And every time you climb in bed
to drift away and dream,

underneath you'll likely hear
little trolls are plotting things.

Put your ear to the ground,
you can listen to them sing.

And since we're talking music,
here's another thing . . .

Those cardboard rolls from paper towels
you use to clean your home?

Don't recycle yet—
    they're really microphones.

And you're a pop star–rock star
with a hip-hop fever,
Chance the Rapper meets Beyoncé
with the moves of a Selena.

Your shower's not just a shower
for the purposes of cleanin'.
It's also a wild jungle
in the middle of rainy season.

That toolbox is your laboratory
where you use your brainy reason

to build machines that run on steam,
contraptions with chain reactions,

mouse traps, bat hats,
mechanical wings for flappin'.

Yes, the place you call your home is
full of wonder and action.

Those chairs and that blanket
will become a fort
to hide from angry warthogs.

Shhhhh, listen to them snort.

That empty plot is not empty—
it's a basketball court

where you invent new sports like "monkey ball" in funky shorts.

Sidewalk-chalk a mural
of an epic battle of the past . . .

Sharks vs. Submarines
Cowboys vs. Physicians

Jets That Break the Sound Barrier
vs. Powerful Steam Engines!

And did you know those people
you live with
who seem to have the answers?

They're not just caretakers,
they're also soulful dancers,
rhymers and painters,
comedians and actors,
writers of books with multiple
chapters!

Which means . . .

you were born creative.
Imagination is your mission.
Wherever you call home . . .
is a canvas for your visions.